MW01100316

counting

comic

history puzzle

electronic craft sticker

spot-the-difference

scary

picture

This book belongs to

BEN, Bella, and...

For Gail and for Friendly,
her fondly remembered dog

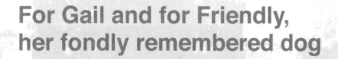

First published in Great Britain in 2015 by Oxford University Press

ISBN 978-1-338-11230-6

12 11 10 9 8 7 6 5 4 3 2 1   16 17 18 19 20 21

Printed in the U.S.A.   40

First Scholastic printing, September 2016

We're in the wrong book!

Richard BYRNE

SCHOLASTIC INC.

Bella and Ben were jumping
down the street, from one side
of the book . . .

to the other.

Then Bella's dog joined in . . .

"Where's my dog?" said Bella.

9 Pencils

"Where are we?" said Ben.

10 Lollipops

"We're in the wrong book!"

9 Pencils

"Well, let's jump back into the right book," said Ben.

But they jumped into . . .

10 Lollipops

. . . somebody else's COMIC book!

Yikes!

Eeek!

"We're trying to get back to our own book," explained Ben and Bella.

"We know someone who can help," said Mouse. "Follow us."

Ben and Bella described their book to the lovely librarian.

"It has tall buildings . . ."

". . . and an enormous dog."

"I know the book," she said.

"It's through there."

HISTORY BOOKS

"I hope she's right," said Bella.

"What does it all mean?" asked Ben.

"I think it says 'Walk this way,'" said Bella.

But things just got more and more puzzling.

And when Bella thought she had found a path that would lead them back to their book . . .

. . . instead it led them to the door of an old cottage in the middle of the woods. Ben and Bella went inside . . .

where an odd-looking lady invited them to stay for dinner. "Thank you, but we really must get back to our own book," said Bella. Ben thought he could see a way back.

Suddenly, Ben and Bella were in a book full of instructions. "I suppose we could follow them," said Bella.

1. Take a piece of rectangular paper.

It doesn't have to be this huge!

2. Fold it in half.

3. Fold a top corner toward the center.

4. Fold the other corner.

5. Fold up the flap at the bottom.

6. Turn over and repeat.

7. Fold both corners of the flap inward.

8) Turn over and repeat.
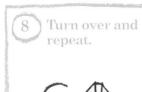

9) Hold the bottom-center fold of each side and pull outward.
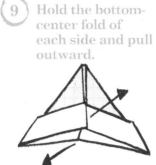

10) Press flat.

11) Fold the bottom triangle up.
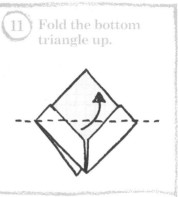

12) Turn over and repeat.

13) Hold the bottom-center fold of each side and pull outward. Press flat.
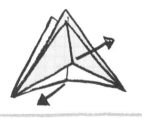

14) Hold the top-outer corners and pull outward.
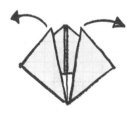

15) Your boat is ready to sail!

Please help me blow the boat off the page!

"Book ahoy!" said Ben.

"The WRONG book ahoy!" grumbled Bella. "And now we're stuck in it!"

So they stuck themselves in a hot-air balloon as it lifted up, up, and away.

The balloon landed
in just the right spot . . .

THIS WAY

for spotting a
very helpful sign.

And they both jumped through
the monster-shaped hole.

"Yay!" said Bella.
"We're back in our book!"

When Ben and Bella came back to fix the hole in their book, there was no sign of the monster.

"Thank goodness!" said Bella. "Now, where's my dog?"